Danse, a Dark Tale of Macabre

B.A.D.

The Ballad of...

The Rat King

This world is filled with unimaginable beauty... and unfathomable horrors. Countless creatures and critters, both powerful and frail, prowl and skitter about its surface.

But the Rat, however, cursed into the lowest caste of existence, is indifferent to it all. They can only observe the world from below and watch its constant cycles of action play out above them— forever in their sight…yet never within their reach.

This Rat in particular, was a mother, pregnant with thirteen fetuses floating about her womb.

Unbeknownst to her and even the universe itself, one of these thirteen fetuses was destined for greatness the likes of which no other rat had ever achieved before.

Soon, the thirteen fetuses were born— becoming
the thirteen infants.

And among them was the future Rat King,
though his crown had yet to be fashioned,
and his deserved revere was withheld by the
premature naivety of others.

The Rat King experienced no special treatment during his upbringing. In fact, he was dealt a hand of the complete opposite.

His brothers and sisters shunned him, and his mother neglected even the basics of nurturing him with her milk. He had nothing, was nothing, and left all alone with only rocks to feed on.

He acquired a chip in his tooth from the feasting on rocks, and a chip on his shoulder from his abandonment. The Rat King, a true rat among rats, was left with nothing in this world except for a slow and festering hate.

However, the infant Rat King turned this hate back towards the world and everything that occupied it. He refused to buckle under its impartial position, and instead, sought to become a ruling player in it.

He chose to make the choices... and to choose the damned.

The unloving family who gave him no
affection were the first to face his judgment,
and by the crushing weight of a boulder—
the very rocks he fed on...

...the mother and siblings
parted with their souls.

This first act of bloodshed was the catalyst to the Rat King's metamorphosis. And as time passed and the Rat King grew older...

...his journey would only continue in a similar malevolent fashion, crafting the very structure of his crown.

And so, the matured Rat King now found himself traveling amongst a scenery of tall grass.

While on this path, he encountered a frog who croaked a tune of sorrows. "Sad Frog, sad Frog, why do you cry?" asked the Rat King.

"Water has become scarce and my own pond is now dwindling away. If I do not find a new one soon, then I too shall dry up and perish" answered the Frog.

"Allow me to help, sad Frog, since
you are bound to that pond.
Perhaps I can find you a new
home where the water is abundant"
said the Rat King.

"Sad Frog, sad Frog!" said the Rat King, "Beyond this tall grass lies another pond, far larger and more bountiful than your current one. Take the leap and find your refuge!"

And so the frog bounded over the tall grass and into his new home.

But it were lies that spilt from the Rat King's lips, as only twisted patches of thorns sat on the other side of the tall grass— now painted in red from the sad Frog's demise.

And so, with another soul added to his collection, the Rat King continued on his merry way.

Along his journey, the Rat King stumbled upon a tired
Hedgehog mothering her three children.

"Tired Hedgehog, tired Hedgehog, why do you sigh?" asked the Rat King.

"My children need my nurturing hand, however, I've found no time to acquire food for myself" answered the tired Hedgehog.

"I know what it's like to be hungry, I once fed only on rocks. I'll watch over your children during your leave so you may find food for yourself" said the Rat King.

And so with great thanks, the tired Hedgehog left the Rat King with her children to search for food.

But upon her return with a belly now full, she discovered
her children had perished, and that the Rat King too bore
a full stomach.

With fleeting feet that scurried speedily,
the Rat King fled the scene as his
stomach digested three more souls to his
collection.

But it was not too long before he was stopped in his
tracks by a large wall of scales.

Then, a voice crept up from behind him, whispered and hoarse it spoke, "Tiny Rat, tiny Rat, why did you run to your death?"

The Rat King sat himself upon a large rock and answered the snake, "Silly Snake, silly snake, I did not run to my death. Rather, I ran from my part in it. But if you insist this is my end, then by all means, please swallow me whole."

In a snap faster than
lighting, a crack faster
than a whip…

…the Snake lunged
its open mouth at the
Rat King.

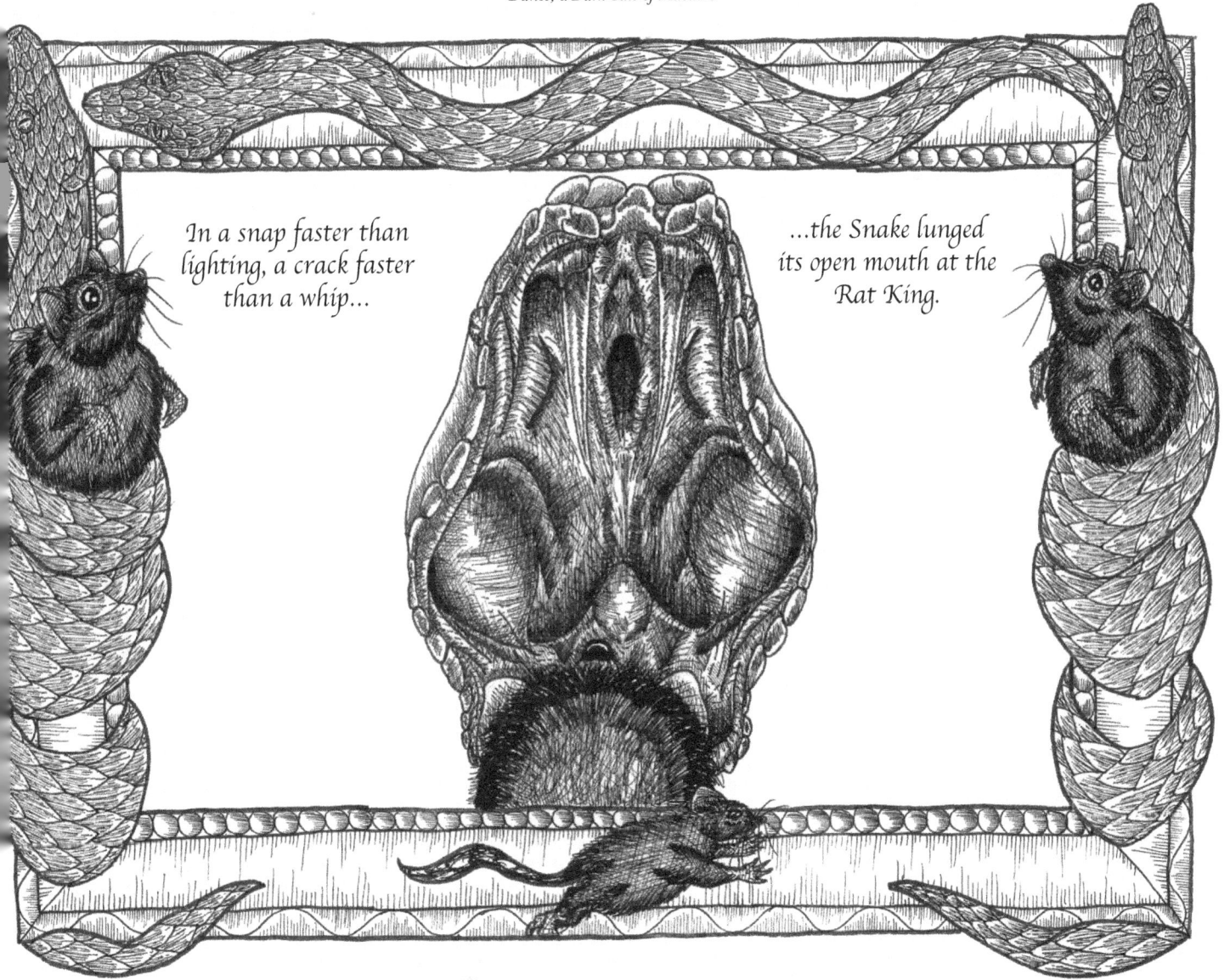

Eyes wide and full of shock, the Snake noticed that its mouth was stuck open halfway down the rock.

And from within its jaws forced wide open, the Rat King slithered his way out from its grasp.

"I am not your prey and I am not your lesser, filthy reptile" said the Rat King, "Only I know how to feast on rocks, so stay there and rot while you choke on your own tongue!"

And with those departing words,
the Rat King continued on his way.

During his travels, the Rat King came across
a glum looking Salamander.

*"Dour Salamander, dour Salamander,
whatever has spoiled your mood?"* asked the
Rat King.

"Water has become scarce in these lands" replied the
Salamander, "And so what was once my pond has now
become a haven for all of the neighboring insects."

"I have an idea to solve your problem" said the Rat King, "Put your head under the water and I will cover your body with mud. That way, no critter nor bug can disturb your peace."

And so the Salamander agreed, only
to realize after that he was trapped in
place, to which the Rat King shouted...

..."Yes, you can
breathe underwater,
but you cannot stay
there forever...

...*If you seek to regain
your freedom, then you
must swallow your pond
dry!*"

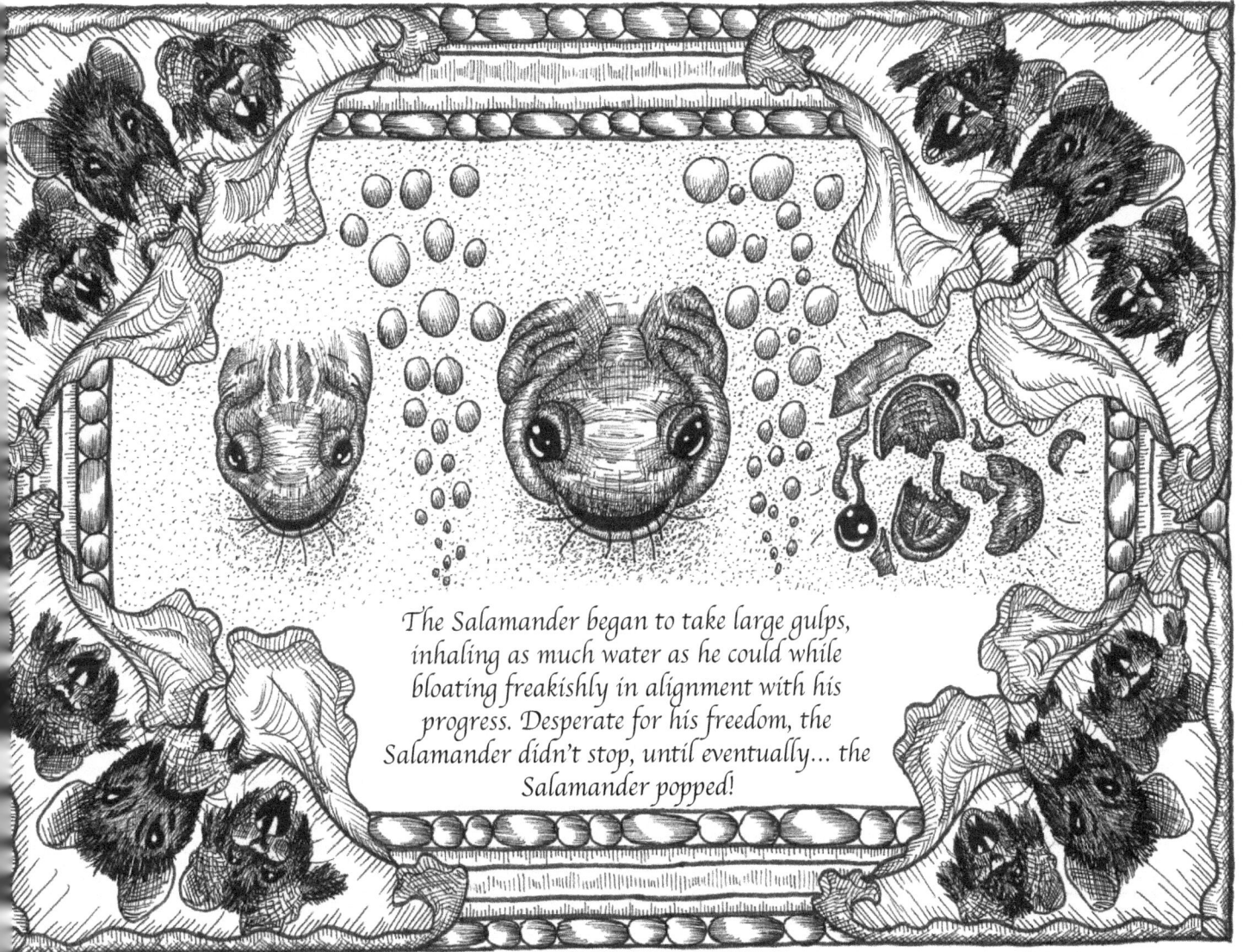

The Salamander began to take large gulps, inhaling as much water as he could while bloating freakishly in alignment with his progress. Desperate for his freedom, the Salamander didn't stop, until eventually... the Salamander popped!

With a trophy of souls now harbored by the Rat King, he proudly strutted along his merry way.

That is, until a monstrous Pig presented itself in front of his path.

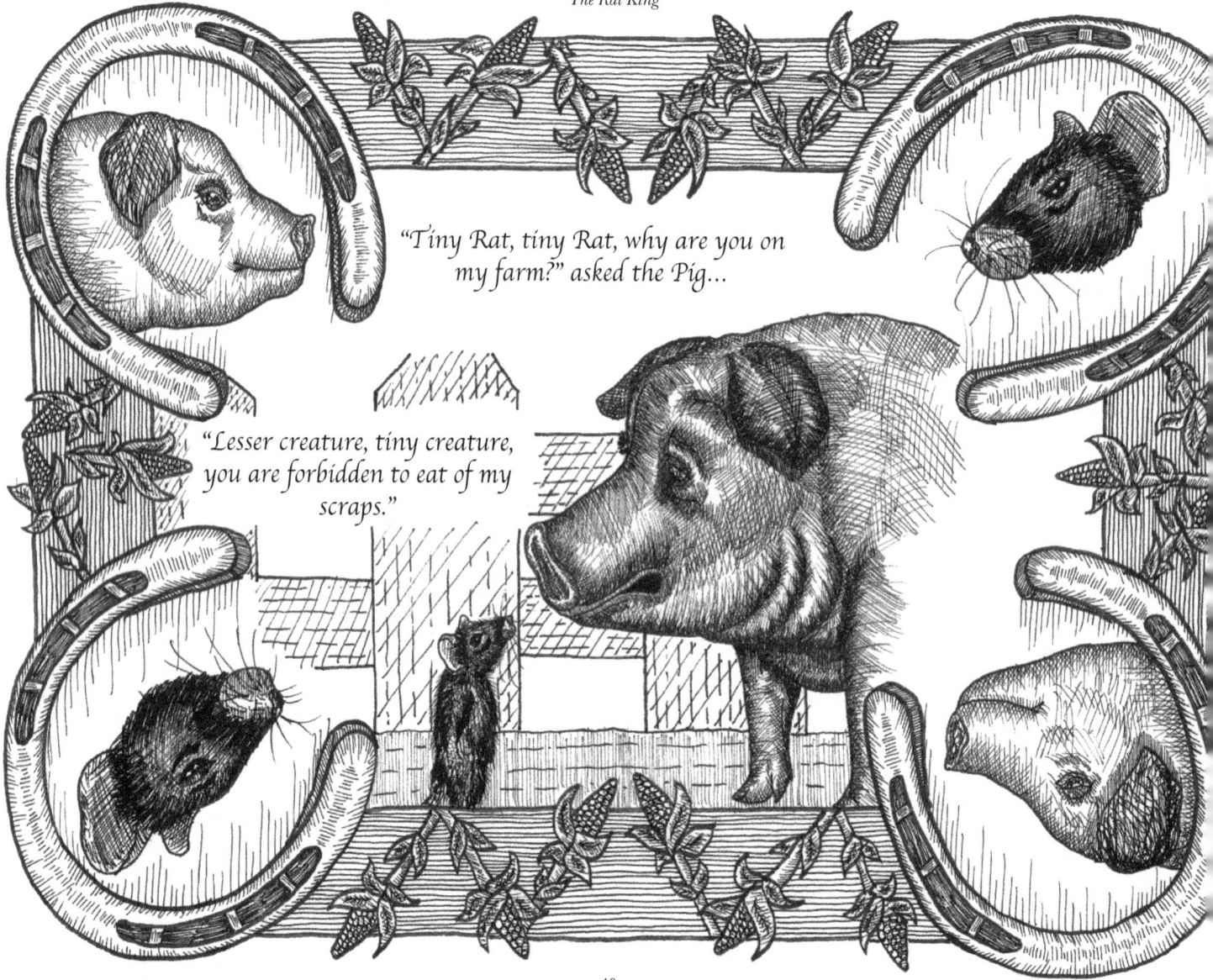

"Tiny Rat, tiny Rat, why are you on my farm?" asked the Pig...

"Lesser creature, tiny creature, you are forbidden to eat of my scraps."

40

Disgruntled by the Pig's demeaning tongue, the Rat King convinced the gluttonous animal to follow him to a secret that he knew of... a secret he wished to share with the Pig.

"It's inside this barn, giant Pig, the secret I wish to show you" said the Rat King...

..."Although I am surprised your superior nose never told you of this sooner."

And upon seeing the contents hidden within the barn, the Pig's face morphed into one of true horror.

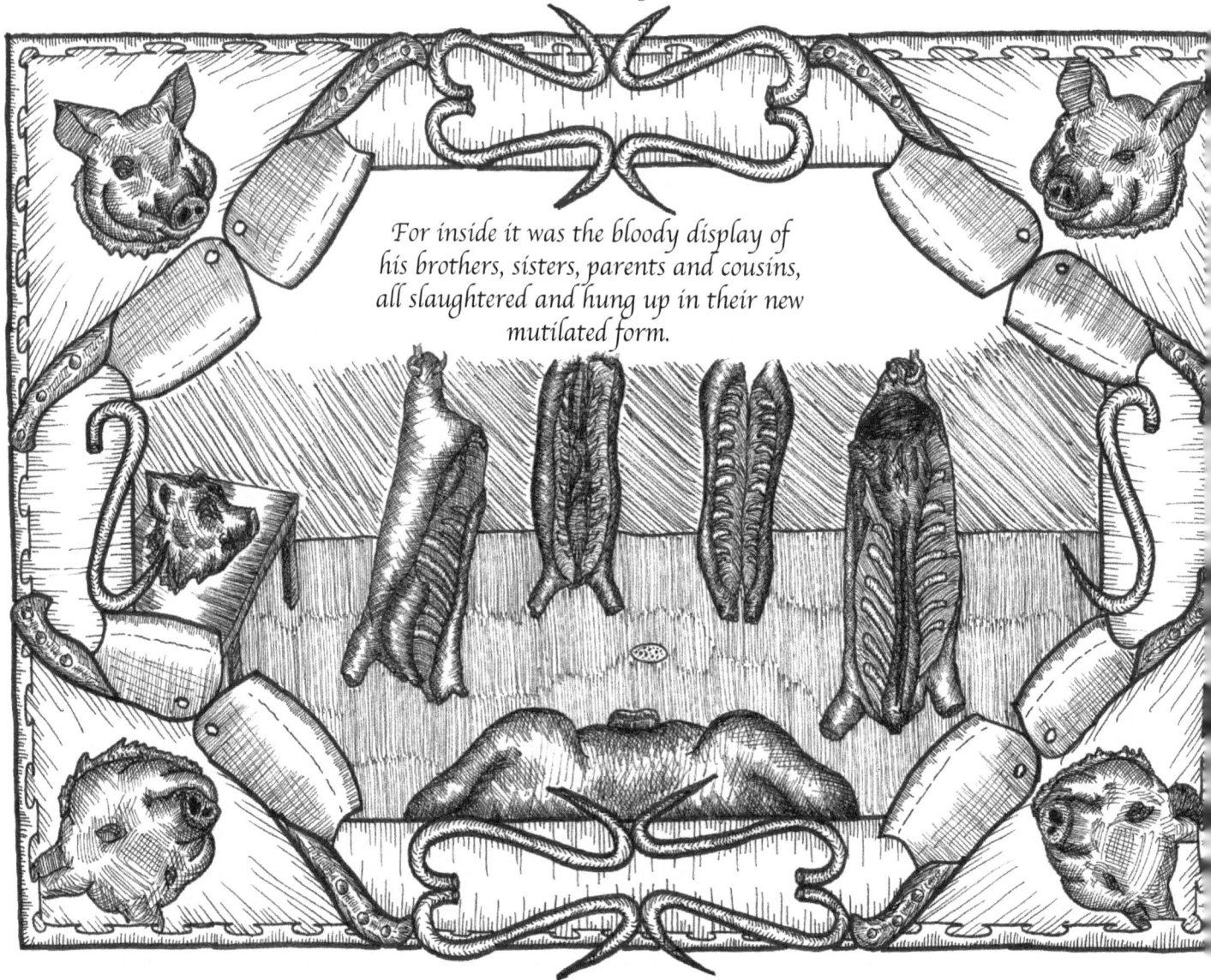

For inside it was the bloody display of
his brothers, sisters, parents and cousins,
all slaughtered and hung up in their new
mutilated form.

"I need not kill you myself, loathful Pig, for your fate is already sealed" said the Rat King...

..."You think you are mighty for being close to the Humans, but really you are damned for it!"

The Rat King left the traumatized Pig behind him, and didn't look back as he continued on his journey.

But then a new obstacle presented itself before the Rat King's path, one much different from his previous encounters. It was a Human, the gods of the food chain, the pinnacle of superiority in the animal world.

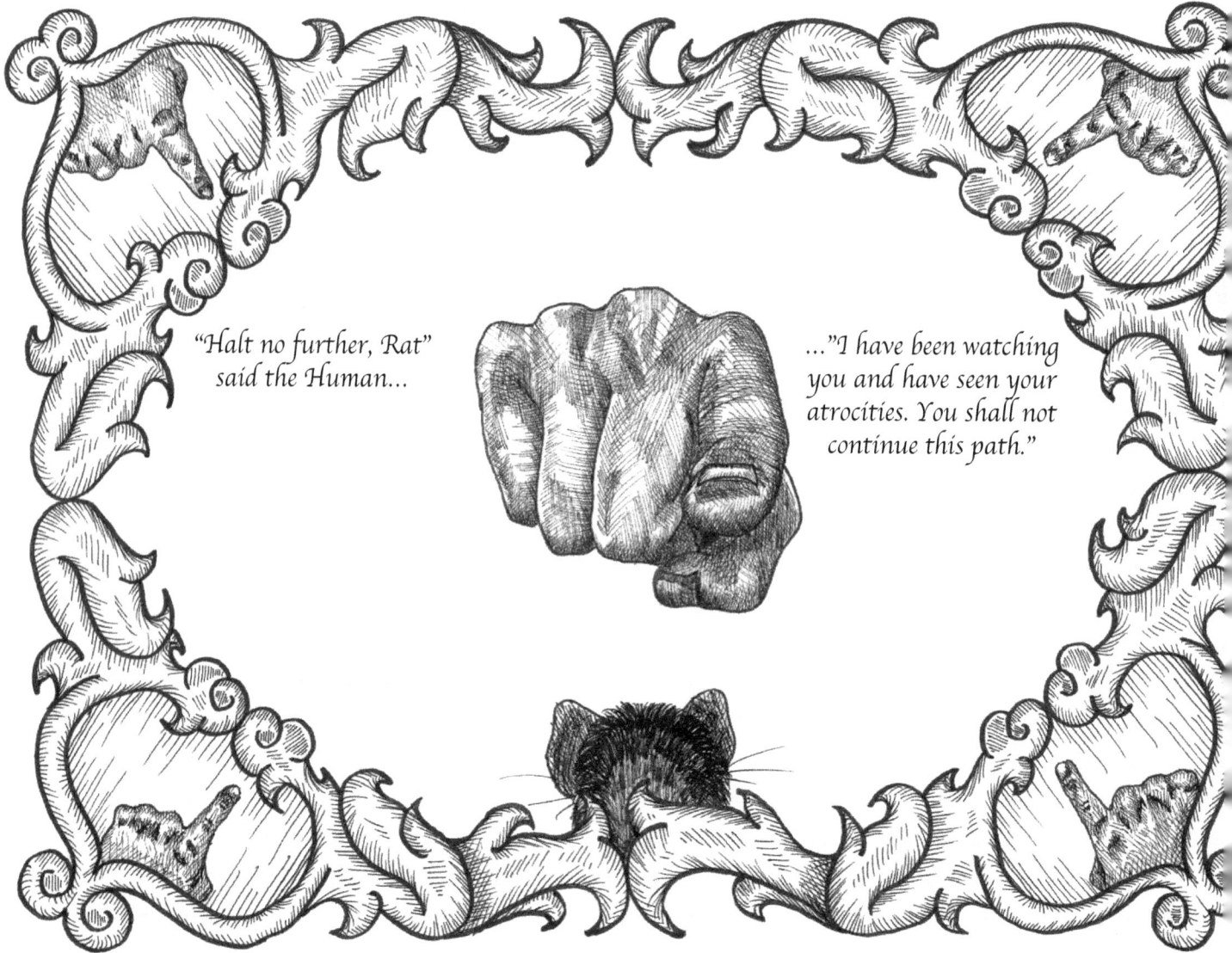

"Halt no further, Rat" said the Human...

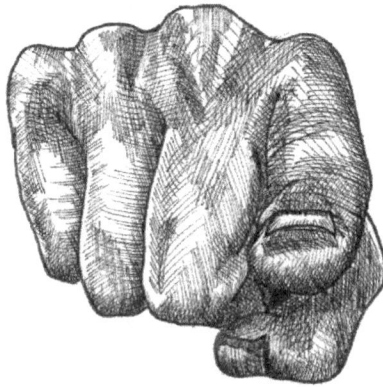

..."I have been watching you and have seen your atrocities. You shall not continue this path."

"You have been watching my journey and find fault in my ways, yet only decide to stop me now when you could have stopped me previously?" questioned the Rat King...

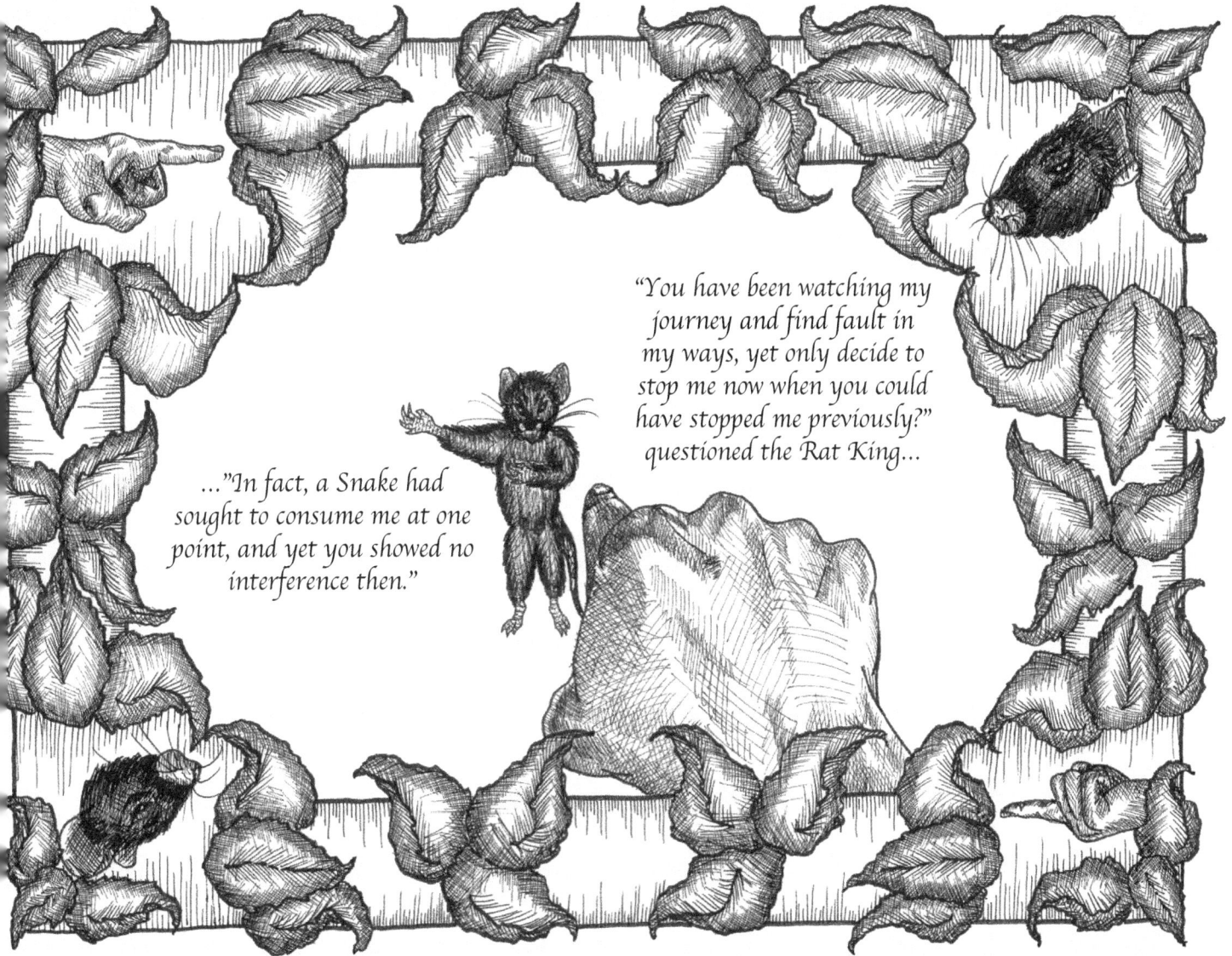

..."In fact, a Snake had sought to consume me at one point, and yet you showed no interference then."

"You false gods bear your false morals while laying judgement down on all that is beneath your brow, yet even the very shoes you walk this earth with are strung from the leather of a life you have slaughtered."

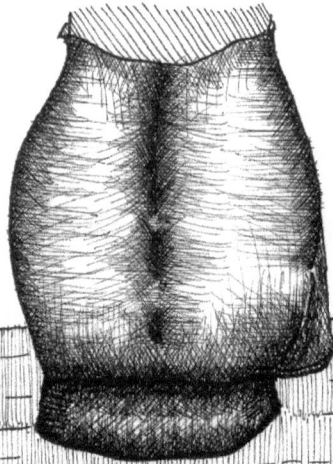

"However, I have earned my crown— unhindered by the lowly curse inherited by my kin. Are your true eyes not open? Can you not see the crown of bones upon my head, and the souls from which they were stripped? You may be a God to us in our world, but I... I am the Rat King!"

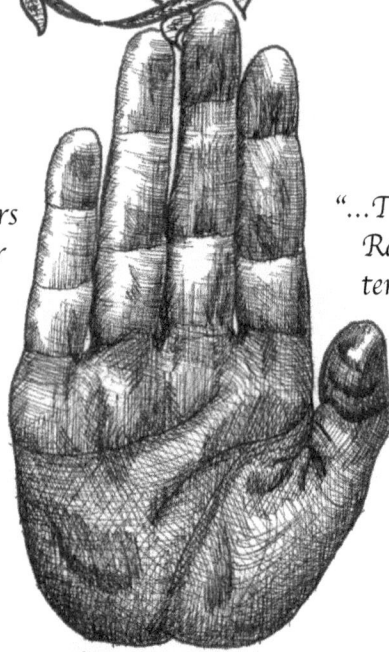

"Enough!" said the Human, "I'll have no ears for you nor any of your preconceived truths…"

"…This ends here and now, Rat. Begone with your terror upon the world."

The Human began to reach down for the Rat King,
entering the world of animals and critters, with an aura
of death awaiting his grasp.

The Rat King sensed his mortality in this moment. Though he could evade predators that desired his body's nourishment, and though he could use his cunning wit to lead a fellow prey to their demise... none of that would work on a human.

Knowing his death was inescapable, the Rat King made a world changing choice in his last decision...

...He sacrificed his soul and twisted his tail, corrupting the very essence of his being into a foul plague of existence.

And when the Human picked him up, the Rat King bore one last smile of deviance...

...Before biting the Human in the final
moment of his life.

The Rat King was now dead and no more, yet his greatest feat had only just begun. The true legend of the Rat King — the one which the entire world has come to know as his deathly terror— blossomed in the black blood that now spread and plagued within this Human's veins.

Bells would come to ring over the countless deaths that followed... but if you ask a Rat, those bells chimed their music for the passing of their King.

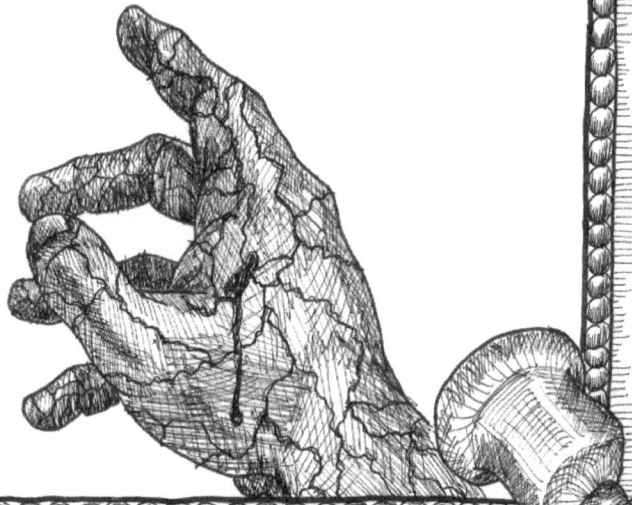

The End

CPSIA information can be obtained
at www.ICGtesting.com
Printed in the USA
BVHW021001130921
616658BV00005B/313